Published by Ad Hoc Fiction.
www.AdHocFiction.com

Purchasing Information:
Paperback available from www.AdHocFiction.com
E-book available from all usual outlets.

Printed in the United Kingdom.
First Printing 2019.

ISBN paperback 978-1-912095-53-7
ISBN e-book 978-1-912095-52-0

With gratitude to Suzanne Clements for creating the cover artwork.

All That Is Between Us

K.M. Elkes

For Michelle

Praise For *All That Is Between Us*

'K.M. Elkes writes like a fallen angel, making the ordinary divine. Tender, visceral, and tough as diamonds, his work cuts every heartbreak into a shining jewel. *All That Is Between Us* finds light in the darkest of places. Though the world may not always be pretty, his characters seek beauty in the connections passing through their lives. This is breath-taking flash fiction at its finest. A book that deserves to be read again and again.'
~ ANGELA READMAN, author of *Something Like Breathing*

'This is fiction of clarity and depth; K.M. Elkes brings a Cheeveresque emotional punch to his stories, married to a sweet, left-of-field insight that is all his own. These are moving, complex, intelligent stories, written in radiant prose. *All That Is Between Us* is a masterclass in the heart-jolting satisfaction of great flash fiction.'
~ NUALA O'CONNOR, author of *Joyride to Jupiter*

'The insightful and disarmingly honest stories in this debut collection shimmer with quirky brilliance, shining a fresh light on how messy it feels to feel. They succeed precisely where the characters' connections fail, demonstrating how relationships can both exacerbate and heal the lifetime ache of being alone. Haunting and funny, these bitter-sweet tales show how even the most secure love can drive us mad.'

~ Meg Pokrass, author of *Alligators At Night*

'I could dazzle you with well-chosen superlatives or make clumsy attempts to sum up K.M. Elkes' work, but really what I want to say is: This collection is so good. So very, very good. Whoever you are, whatever you like to read, you need these stories in your life.'

~ Tania Hershman, author of *Some Of Us Glow More Than Others*

'These stories explore the vagaries of human relationships with an uncanny, algorithmic precision. They linger in the heart and mind long after the final page. Truthful, revelatory, and beautifully written, *All That Is Between Us* is a collection you'll want to read and reread. Highly recommended.'

~ Kathy Fish, author of *Wild Life: Collected Works*

'K.M. Elkes explores the mechanics of relationships with both sober realism and a sparkling, dry wit. This book is a string of perfect moments. Whether it examines friends, lovers or families, each flash lingers in the reader's mind like a particularly bright, perfectly polished gem.'
~ SOPHIE VAN LLEWYN, author of *Bottled Goods*, longlisted for the Women's Prize For Fiction

'This collection is crammed with powerful and moving images…In my favourite piece, Extremities, a chainsaw accident leaves you thinking less about the victim and more about his severed hand, lying alone in the woods, fingers grasping at nothing. The stories move together like a murmuration of texts, each slipping in and out of the other, making every fragment part of a whole experience, almost as if it were a shattered novel you've found on the floor and are trying to piece together.'
~ DAVID GAFFNEY, author of *All The Places I've Ever Lived*

'In K.M. Elkes's fictional world, bruised dads turn up out of the blue to take their lonely kids on disappointing zoo visits, then return to claim back a wardrobe from their estranged wives. The wardrobe's been made in Johnny Cash fashion, out of bits stolen from a mill. As it is dragged to the

dad's car, the wardrobe 'gouges a black trail through the lawn'. These razor-sharp stories have left a trail like that in me, too. They are full of bruised beauty, and they will stay in your heart. A brilliant book.'
~ DAVID SWANN, author of *The Privilege Of Rain*

Contents

Parents
and
Children

Could Have, Would Have, Should Have

You could have cried at the birth. You could have kissed your wife's cracked lips and said: 'You did it, Tess.'

You could have been amazed at the pureness of nails, a nostril's arc, the creases of plump hands gripping like tiny, soft-shelled crabs.

In a few more years, you could have ended a sentence '...so that's why rain is wet, Emily.' You could have made up any old explanation, as long as you got to say her name.

You could have stood at the window (it would have been a bright day), her on a chair, tiptoed, studying the genius of the roadsweeper's whirling brush outside.

She would have waved, said: 'Look, see the clean' and you would have said, 'Honey, it's see *how* clean' and she would have mouthed a silent 'how' in a way that would have made your throat ache.

You could have gone to Aqualand and watched her churning water in bright pink armbands, a plastic bobble in her hair. You could have talked to the father of a boy she plays with, shyly splashing.

You would have agreed to meet him later, for a pint and the usual chat about sons and daughters, family colds, the hundredth bedtime reading of familiar Grimm tales. You would have stayed till closing time and thought you had made a friend.

You would have said to your wife that children are maps, an A–Z of Heaven and Hell. She would have said: 'David, just be grateful.'

You should have stayed at home today, not been in a car with the heater on, waiting in a layby for your spare phone to ring. You should have remembered how Friday is bad for lovers. You should have said, when you had the chance: 'We're out of choices...'

You should have turned off the radio, not listened to the voice telling you, as if it meant nothing at all, that there is snow, coming slowly from the east.

Biological

Gabriel arranges to meet the woman at the train station on a cold November day. He cannot use the same words the adoption people used – 'birth mother'. Instead she is 'the woman'. The woman who gave birth to him. The woman who gave him away.

He arrives an hour before her train is due and sits with a folded newspaper in the waiting room. He glances at his watch, at his polished shoes, at a poster advertising cheap holidays. It has a picture of a smiling toddler saddled on his mother's hip. Somewhere a radiator clanks and beats like a mechanical heart.

When her train arrives, Gabriel goes out and stands by the ticket barrier as agreed, unsure where to put his hands. The woman, Dorothy, wears a peacock blue coat and fumbles a ticket from her purse. She looks older than he expected, smaller.

When she sees him, Dorothy nods and says: 'You've got my features, then. That's a start.'

They go to the Black and White Café, just a street away from the station because Dorothy cannot walk so well. It's a small place of grubby tablecloths and plastic flowers, smelling of gammon and vinegared chips. They order coffees and a couple of chocolate éclairs from under a glass dome.

There is no elegant way to eat the cakes, and they both dab at smears of cream and chocolate at the sides of their mouths, saying nothing. Their coffees steam. They listen as two old men argue over a crossword clue.

'Am I what you was expecting?' Dorothy asks.

Gabriel doesn't know what to say that would sound nice, so he asks: 'I just want to know. Why did you give me up?'

There are cigarettes and long nights in her voice as she tells the story. There's singing and gin, a girl who met a boy in the alley behind her home and climbed up the hill overlooking the town. There's a sixteen-year-old who gave herself up in a sandy hollow crowned with wind-burned grass. There are cold hospital corridors ringing with footsteps.

Dorothy finishes, blows her nose and wipes her eyes. 'Anyhow,' she says, 'I never asked what's it you do for work?'

'A biology teacher,' he says.

'Fancy,' she says.

Gabriel doesn't tell her it's all so-fucking-what these days. He doesn't mention the nights he has wished to open himself like a lab specimen, reach in and pull out his heart, study it, glistening in his hands.

'How did you feel, seeing me again at the station?' he says at last.

'In truth, I'm glad it's out the way,' she says.

'I just don't know what to think,' he says.

Dorothy points a sharp-knuckled finger at him, crooked with arthritis. 'Ah now, see, you get that from me.'

He gets up and goes to the counter, orders two more coffees, both milk, no sugar. He wonders if Dorothy has eczema, acid reflux, pins and needles in the shoulder, if she's restless when there's a bright moon, gets headaches before a storm. Feels emptied out.

When he goes back, careful to avoid any spills, they ask each other questions, some at least, not always the right ones. Gabriel wonders if the impression left of each will be a half-likeness, but not the whole. Eventually their conversation slows, cools, forms a skin.

'Just so you know, you're from the Lancashire Thomases,' she says. 'There are cousins of mine, ours, who have a big factory somewhere. Manchester, I think.'

They watch the wind blow a man's umbrella inside out. Cups clink, someone behind them coughs and time ticks over.

'I'd best get on,' she says. 'Otherwise I'll miss the cheap train.'

At the platform, Dorothy reaches up and twists out a loose thread from his coat.

'There, that's better,' she says, and for the first time smiles.

When the train arrives, she turns to go, then turns back: 'It were such a long time ago, son.'

He feels as though he has reached the bottom of a well, looking up to see the sun, the moon, stars passing.

'Will you give me a call?' she asks. And Gabriel sees, finally, a frail old woman, a proud coat wearer, a digger of tickets from purses, a coffee drinker. A young, frightened girl sitting in a shadow, waiting.

'Of course,' he wants to say, if only, if only he could speak.

Sisyphus and the Black Holes

Nobody explains how there are five stages of grief – having kids in the first place, the experimental pissing phase, the era of sticky door handles, pocket money as a form of quantitative easing, and finally acceptance.

The midwife doesn't tell you she slaps them so they *stay* angry.

They don't reveal the intricacies of compromise. You are left to discover, by accident, that a Sunday newspaper supplement can still be enjoyed, at length, in a cloakroom smelling of shit and feet. Or that on nights when you reveal the stars in all their glory, the firmament and all of that, it is always good to have a moon (two would be better) in your back pocket.

They don't use the words Sisyphean or Herculean. They don't reference Greek mythology at all, not even mentioning Hydras in armbands, snapping at attempts to remove them from holiday pools.

You will discover, alone, the unbearable tension of rainy school runs, the language of door slams, angry exchanges about sweat-pitted cousins, the whole tangle of birthdays, and how, with the addition of hormones, they are whole universes of black holes, swallowing light.

And yet.

Neither do they mention the prick-throated happiness when light lightly covers them, or the smell of their scalps, like a freshly cooked poem.

Or how when they drift to you, and are unexpectedly still, it is as though a breeze has blown a snowflake to your face.

They don't tell you there has never been so much absence, as the absence when they are gone. And that then, only then, will you miss the rock and the hill.

Giraffe High

Dad showed up one slow, hot afternoon while I was playing in the front garden. I hadn't seen him for a year. He was driving a faded red car that sagged on its suspension, and when he wound down the window and called my name, I saw he had two black eyes and a swollen nose.

He lit a cigarette and said I should get in the car because we were taking a trip to the zoo. I hesitated and looked back at the house.

'Sunshine,' he said, 'don't fret about your mum.'

We drove for a while, not saying anything, but I couldn't keep quiet for long, not at that age. 'Those black eyes,' I said. 'You look like a panda bear.'

'Then I'll fit right in at the zoo,' he replied.

We went to watch the monkeys first. While we were there, a tall man in a uniform came up and said smoking was not permitted. Had we not seen the signs? My dad nodded and took a drag, then dropped his cigarette on the ground.

'Sir. It's still burning,' said the tall man.

Dad turned back towards the monkey cage.

'See these chimps, son. Keep watching them – they just love to sling their shit around.'

The tall man bent down then and took the burning cigarette away.

When we got to the giraffes, dad swung me up on his shoulders so I could be giraffe-high, though I was too old, really, for all that. He told me the zoo secretly spent money on specialists who worked at night, washing the giraffes' necks. The really good ones, he said, were promoted to elephant duty, ironing their ears.

I laughed so hard at that I nearly fell. I wrapped my arms around his head to hold on, and my chin rested on the warm piece of scalp where he was thinning out. We stayed like that for a good, long time until he whispered 'ice cream' and lowered me down.

When we got back home, Mum opened the door before I got up the path. She told me I should go straight to my room and wait for her there.

They went at each other for a long time. Then I saw him out of my window, hauling the cedar wardrobe from her bedroom across the front garden, gouging a black trail through the lawn.

He had made that wardrobe himself, with wood stolen from the mill where he worked with my uncle, until they closed the place down. He made the hinges by hand in his shed at night and polished the whole thing until the light bounced off of it like a diamond. Whenever him and my mother went dancing they would both have that sweet scent of cedar on their clothes.

That wardrobe was big and difficult for one person to handle. I wanted to go out and help him, but I could hear my mum in the kitchen, trying to be quiet. So I just stood on top of my toy box, nearly giraffe-high, hoping he'd see me wave.

It took a long time for him to get the wardrobe onto the roof of his old, red car. When he drove away, one of the doors that wasn't lashed down flapped open on a broken hinge. He didn't stop.

The last time I saw my dad, he seemed weather-beaten and taller because he was so thin. Mum had passed away not long after my stepfather, and when I called to let Dad know, he said he wanted to be there for the funeral. That bygones were bygones.

We drove back from the cemetery among a line of cars, the passenger window wound down so he could smoke. We passed by the sawmill, the derelict buildings roofless and rotten, the walls choked by trees and bushes.

'When were you happiest, Dad?' I asked. He didn't hesitate, pointed straight at the old place. He told me Uncle Mike always said they used to looked like tramps coming down the hill from there, covered in dust, their pockets packed with sharp tools.

'Maybe Mikey was right, but we were rich, in our own way. We made something worthwhile,' he said.

He smiled then and looked at me: 'But I guess I didn't quite make it to washing giraffe necks or ironing elephant ears, did I?'

When I took him to the coach station that night, he took his bag from the back seat then leaned down, pulled my head forward and put his palm right where my hair was starting to thin out.

'See,' he said. 'Some things you just can't get away from, sunshine.'

Later, when I was in bed with Mary and it was dark and quiet except for Reuben gurgling on the baby monitor, a memory arrived clear and fresh. I had gone to the hospital with a fever. Dad took me. I could only have been seven or eight years old.

I don't know if it was the fever or not, but the way I remembered it now, he was standing at the foot of my bed, telling the nurse in a quiet voice: 'Please, love. Just remember the boy doesn't like apricots, or porridge or brown bread...'

There was just me, the nurse and my dad, all looking down at his hands as he counted off the list with his thick, calloused fingers.

On a Red-Eye Heading East

Last weekend, Daniel spent 43 hours straight with his daughter Esme. Nearly two whole days. Nearly. Now he is 30,000 feet up on a red-eye heading east, looking at a picture she has posted online – a selfie and the shadow of his face. He is not tagged.

Planes, hotel rooms, quiet corridors in office towers. These are the places where he finds a little time, like a fisherman standing in a fast-flowing river, hoping to hook something beautiful, reel it in, hold it for a while.

He spends these moments 'liking' her uploaded images – the lemon drizzle cake she made, Esme with a ginger-haired girl he doesn't recognise, her new patent-leather shoes. Or typing funny comments about cold feet, hair braids, boys in spectacles; thumbing love into the holy blue glow of the screen, as if a string of 0s and 1s were invisible threads that joined them.

A stewardess, greying and flat-shoed, sees a picture on his laptop. She asks: 'Is she your daughter, sir?'

The picture isn't her, not really, he says. None of it is, the patchwork of messages and posts and the slow, twitching images of video calls.

'Zoom in. Just zoom in and see how pixelated she gets,' he says.

When she turns away wordless, Daniel regrets his candour, the potential rudeness. But later she brings him a whisky, unasked, then leans in and tells him it is on the house. She has kids, is divorced, understands.

After she has moved on he sits quietly, held down by the weight of the laptop and the phone, silent, in his pocket.

Daniel thinks about the weekend just gone. He drove through a blizzard to his ex-wife's house and took Esme back to his too-hot, too-small new place where they scoured raspberry jam straight from the jar and gazed out at the ghost trails left by birds in the snow.

When the weather relented Esme insisted they go out, so they bought a plastic sled and drove out to the hills near the village where he grew up. When they crossed a bridge at the foot of the slopes, Daniel stopped and told Esme about how snow changed the sound of everything.

'Listen to the stream, I mean really listen to it,' he said, and was silent for a long time, until Esme pulled on his hand, said she wanted to have fun.

He watched her sail down the hill, time after time, worrying about the cold and the night and what they should eat when they got back.

Then she said: 'Let's build a snowman' and they worked together, heaving a great ball of snow around the bottom of the hill, a lesser one for the head. He gave up his scarf and his hat and Esme made a face from twigs. When they had finished, she adjusted the cap to a better angle, then patted its belly.

'Looks like you, Dad.'

Against the hum of the plane's engine, Daniel remembers how, as they were leaving, he turned and saw the swathe of grass they had exposed all around the snowman, bright green, incredible in its colour.

He stares out at the vast fields of clouds that stretch, white and unending, to the horizon. He thinks about what lies below.

By now the snowman would have melted and the deep, bright grass would be an unremarkable piece of field. Maybe someone walking there would see a hat and scarf, a pile of twigs. They might wonder, just for a moment, about who left them there and why.

He didn't take a picture of the snowman. Neither did Esme. There had been no profile update, no location marked, no online record uploaded, filed or shared. But when Daniel closes his eyes he can hear the trickle of a stream dulled by snow, the sharp pipe of his daughter's laughter in cold air. He can smell crushed grass and feel the wondrous weight of tiredness in his limbs from carrying his sleeping daughter to bed.

You Wonder How They Sleep

It is 3am, again. You cannot sleep for the same reason you always cannot sleep – one black thought that rises like a starling into an evening sky, before a whole murmuration follows.

You get up, pull on yesterday-smelling clothes, lace your shoes and go downstairs. There was a time when you would have paused outside your daughter's room, ear to the door, just in case she had returned as silently as she left.

The night is still and warm. You walk past the scent of night phlox and honeysuckle from the hermit's garden, past the rainbow shutters of the corner shop. You cross the cobbled square where tree roots have breached the surface, like the backs of whales coming up for air.

You walk on until the All-Night Café announces itself as a smell, of hot pastries and coffee. It is crowded inside, the familiar faces of other nightwakers scattered about, like penitents waiting for confession. There is a free space on a sofa, next to a young woman you have never seen before. When you ask if you can sit, she glances at you, then makes room. She is about the age your daughter would have been.

You sit and let the ache of memory swell and roll until, eventually, the young woman puts down her book, sighs, and leans her head against your shoulder. This is natural. There is a comradeship among the sleepless, an acceptance that convention is redundant. Without each other, there is only the long night folding over you, the counting of stars and the ways you failed.

Eventually, the young woman spools through her story as though she were letting out a fishing line. How she found solace a few days back with two old women in leather skirts who sang karaoke in a bar. How she had to run away from a man who had promised her a job telling tourists about local wine. How there had been a boy, but he was deported. She had given him her mother's wedding ring. She regretted it now.

Then she says: 'I suppose you want to go to bed with me?'

You shake your head and soon after she falls asleep. Exposed behind her ear is a small tattoo in a neat, Gothic font. Just two letters: T and H. The boyfriend you think, or perhaps another man who promised her something else.

She wears a filthy silk coat, torn under the arm. The brush of it against your hands is like the first time touching snow.

Walking home, as dawn crouches on the horizon, you see a fox nose its way through split rubbish bags. Sometimes, on these long nights, when you press your ear against a window to feel the vibrations of trains and the deep, deep breath of the city, you hear a vixen scream and think of your daughter and pull your head from the glass as though it were hot.

The fox looks up and stares directly at you. It blinks and sniffs, then goes about its business until it pads into the shadows with a chicken carcass swaying in its mouth.

You wonder if it has young to feed. You wonder if they are safe in their den. You wonder how they sleep.

Still Warm

The boy sat at the top of the stairs and waited for the smell to reach him. He was familiar with the kitchen scene below – a fat turd of minced pork sausagemeat smoking in a pan. His mother leant over the counter, letting the edge whiten ridges into her palms. The high shriek of the extractor fan, extracting.

Across the landing his father grimaced round a shaving brush, then dipped his razor and drew it down his neck. The boy remembered the noise of stubble against his father's collar when he used to kiss him goodnight. Alive and mysterious, like radio static. His father double-tapped the razor on the sink and toed the bathroom door shut.

The boy slid down three stairs, settled and waited.

Recipe For a Boy's Lunch:
One slice of thin white bread, unbuttered.
Ground pork sausagemeat, fried the colour of night.
A shake or two of ketchup.
One slice of thin white bread, unbuttered.

His mother cried and stared and lay in darkened bedrooms with a damp flannel over her brow because she was a woman of a certain age, his father told him, weak with her nerves. That whatever they did, they were quiet. That they did not disturb. His father said none of this was the boy's fault. Except, the way he said it, it was.

The boy slid again, settled, waited. He idled against the pale ribs of the banisters until he was finally called into the kitchen. Cooking had finished, but the smoke hung about like early morning mist. He remembered, as he always did, to say thank you as the wrapped sandwich was handed to him. It had the weight of a human heart.

His mother wet her fingers and slicked down a rogue lock on the boy's head, then sighed and kissed a cheek and told him to behave himself. She smelled of burnt meat.

Five years hungry, that boy. Yet on his way to school, he took the same care as always, the same love as always, when he fed a neighbour's bin with that wrapped and blackened heart, inedible and still warm.

Swimming Lessons

On Sundays they opened the lake for public swimming. Marion said it would a treat for Alice, but Tom was reluctant, until he remembered being taken there by his own father for swimming lessons.

They packed everything they needed – towels, swimming costumes, sunscreen, repellent. When Alice asked if they were taking a picnic, Tom said:

'You want to mix eating and swimming? Really?'

Marion made sandwiches anyway. She wrapped them in sheets of greaseproof paper, then slid the package carefully into a bag, while Tom watched on. She held the bag on her lap as they drove to the lake through the heavy, silent afternoon.

It was already crowded when they arrived, and Tom had to haggle for a small patch of grass between two big, noisy families. This kind of thing would never have happened if his father were still alive. Thomas Senior had been someone, a man of note in the town – these people would have made space for him without the little tuts and puffs of air as they moved their picnic blankets.

Once they had settled, Alice changed into her swimming costume and began playing with a bright green plastic ball, wary of the sharp metallic ring it gave when it bounced. A boy with a slick of blond hair came over to watch. Each time the ball slipped away from Alice he chased it and brought it back. They began to play catch, Alice giggling as the boy threw the ball ever higher.

'Keep your eyes open, Alice, as you receive the ball,' Tom shouted.

The children played on, but Alice was awkward in her movements, the ball veering away when she tried to throw it hard.

'Push your elbows in when you throw, Alice, like I demonstrated,' said Tom.

'Just let her be,' said Marion. 'She needs to learn things on her own. She won't with you always at her.'

Tom stood with his hands on his hips, squinting out across the packed slopes. The afternoon was thick with the loudness of children and the smell of food. He sat down and opened his book. He read for a while, all the time worrying at the corner of the bookmark with his nail. Then he carefully placed it between the appropriate pages and looked at his wife.

'Why, Marion, do I get such fucking hostility all the time?' he asked.

'For God's sake, not here and now,' said Marion.

He lay on his back and closed his eyes, heard the green ball ping as it bounced. He heard Alice's laughter, high-pitched against the murmur of the lake crowd. Then he felt Marion get up, her sandals slapping against her feet as she walked away towards the sound of their daughter. The ball pinged again and he listened to his wife's own high-pitched laugh as she joined in the game.

Tom jumped to his feet.

'Right then, young lady, I think it's time you had your swimming lesson.'

He strode over to Alice, swept her up, walked the few paces to the edge of the lake and heaved her into the water. He heard Marion gasp, but didn't turn around. Instead he stood, arms crossed, watching Alice resurface, flapping wildly.

'That's the way,' he called out to Alice. 'Sink or swim.'

'What the hell are you doing?' shouted one of the men who had moved to make space for him.

'I know what's best for my daughter,' said Tom. 'What worked for me will work for her.'

Marion pushed past him, but he grabbed her arm and held her, nails digging into the skin, feeling it yield like a peach.

'Just stop, Marion, and take a look. See, she's doing it. She's doing it.'

Alice had managed to surface again and somehow, slapping the water with the flat of her hands, head arched and eyes squeezed shut, she was making her way to the edge of the lake.

'You idiot!' said Marion.

She wrenched herself from his grip and reached down to help Alice from the water. Pulling her onto the grass slope and into her arms, rocking as the girl shivered and wept.

'That's how Daddy learned to swim, sweetheart,' he said. 'So well done you.'

Alice turned away, pushed her face into her mother, and for a moment Tom saw her as a baby again, searching for a nipple, before mother and daughter walked back up to the picnic blanket and sat together huddled under towels.

In a few moments the afternoon began to reassert itself, the loudness and the heat and the smell of food. And no one paid Tom any notice as he stepped to the edge of the slope, flexed up onto his toes and launched himself into the water, then kicked hard, just as his father had taught him. He had no idea how deep the lake was, but he kept pushing down into the darkness, legwork clean and efficient, pushing down and down and down, willing the pain in his ears and the hurt of his lungs to grow.

My Father, Who Ate a Tree

My father ate an apple tree. All of it – fruit, leaves, branches, even the trunk. It was to teach us a lesson about denial, or perseverance. Or something like that. It killed him in the end.

My childhood was only him, myself, my mother. Sometimes there was joy, like Field Stroll or Radio Hour or Hair Cleaning Day, when Mother washed mine, then me hers, in an afternoon kitchen filled with the splash of water and the draw of a brush through damp hair.

Other times we sneaked into the garden, plucking fruit from the old apple tree to feed the donkey in a neighbouring field. My father hated that animal. When it brayed too hard or long, he chased it with a stick, though he never landed a blow.

The day he caught us feeding the donkey, my father vowed to eat the tree, to end our wickedness. He fetched a stool and his sharpest saw, filled a bucket with salt water to soften the wood, then sat and began.

He had devoured most of the branches when people began to come to see him eat, until it became a pilgrimage to witness the miracle tree eater. My mother hid us away at first, but in time grew used to the crowds. She sold them food and drink and homemade packets of apple seeds.

My father ignored them all. His teeth were worn and blunted by his labour and he ate so slowly and deliberately that the visitors grew bored and went away.

Eventually, near the end, he stopped coming back into the house. At night he slept curled round the bark-stripped stump of the tree and during the day shouted obscenities. We learned new songs from the radio and sang them all day to drown out the noise.

When my father died, choked by the apple tree's final root, we buried him in the hole he had left in the garden, then moved on to a new life. I returned to the old place just once, years later. The house had fallen into disrepair. But in the garden was a young tree, bright with apples and the old donkey plump and quiet in its shade.

Three Kids, Two Balloons

We are late, again, because the eldest tore a wing off the youngest's dress and the middle one refused her shoes. There's a nip to the air and a cellar-black sky and, as I magnificently predicted on the journey down, this 'communidy fête' is a dismal, nearly over, affair.

The face painters have knocked off early and the only thing that lingers in the food tent is a stink of onions and the buttery tang of trodden grass. The children are wailing for entertainment, but the stage holds a thin girl reading poetry with the voice of a cracked oboe.

Then we see the Balloon Man, a short rump of a fella trailing two last globes, the runts of the litter, the last-chance salooners.

'We'll take them,' says the wife and gives up twice the money she ought. Transferred to other hands, the two balloons sink further on their strings, like geriatric dogs settling in hot gutters.

'Now then,' she says, and hands them to me. The children look up like open-beaked birds, expectant of an equal share.

'Now then what?' I say. 'How does this work?'

'Just… keep a hold of them for now.'

I wish for a moment we had arrived early, so I could throw cash at Balloon Man for his whole stock and let myself go, drifting up, hearing faint voices: 'My daddy can fly. My daddy is a spaceman. See him soar.'

But I know I would look down at my wife's disapproving face, see her pull up a sock or wipe a nose, knowing I'd let go soon enough, because I don't have the strength to cling on.

At home, the children look at each other, then the balloons. There are knives in those looks, howitzers, the shelling of their respective positions will be thunderous and sustained.

Who gets the balloons, they shout. Want mine, they shout. Not fair, they shout. Step up to the plate, Daddy, they mean.

'Here's the thing,' I say. 'These two poor balloons are missing the third one. Just like you Katie and Anna would miss Jack, or Jack and Katie would miss Anna. Or any other combination thereof.'

I'm flagging already, but they sit, prepared to go with this for a while. I look to my wife. She takes things on. She busies them writing out a little card, a plea for a missing balloon. They are liberal with glitter and glue, then add some extra, then brighten the table, floor and cat.

We go out into the garden and tether the balloons to the card and then to each other. There is a degree of solemnity in the dusk air. The five of us gather and release the balloons, and the five of us see them drift away, wobbling, directionless and odds-on certain to rupture on a rooftop or flail into some half-distant wires and pop in an electric fizz.

But for a few brief seconds they rise. They soar. And we are a quiet family, watching them go.

Dissolved

Coming back to pick up a few last things, I knocked and waited on the step, thinking how home wasn't the right word for this place any more. Vanessa let me in, proffered a cheek and asked about my journey, the bad weather, work.

In the kitchen we divided crockery and cutlery into cardboard boxes. Standing on a chair I reached up to scour the back of one high cupboard and found a plastic mug, cartoon red with a picture of a bright yellow duck. I held it for a while, then passed it to Vanessa, who wiped off the dust and placed it in the box marked 'Charity'.

The rain fell for an hour, then two, then more. We stood and smoked at the back door, watched a sheen of water run down the road. From it, a tributary flowed beneath the bottom gate, swirling round the skinny legs of the garden swing.

'That thing was cheap. It's gone rusty,' Vanessa said. 'We should have taken it down at the time.'

'And do what with it?' I asked.

The radio announced flood warnings. Trains were cancelled. Roads were awash, rivers had burst their banks. Hunker down, said the weatherman.

We found a few old sandbags out in the shed and did our best to block the doors, then unpacked a pair of cups and made tea.

'Why do they cope better with bad weather in other countries?' Vanessa asked.

'Do they?' I said, 'Maybe they are just more used to it. Maybe they expect it more than we do.'

'I was thinking about New York.'

'For bad weather?'

'For a job. A new start.'

She switched on the television. News helicopters whirled over fields of choppy water and submerged trees. There were pictures of a family on the roof of their shed, waving.

'Or maybe volunteering somewhere,' said Vanessa. 'A refugee camp. Helping children.'

'Sure, Nessie. And you've thought about living in France and keeping goats. And you've thought about going to County Sligo to find your lost family. And now these,' I said.

'You know what I mean,' she said.

We went upstairs, lay on the bed and listened to the rain run through gutters. Half-asleep and heavy-lidded, Vanessa whispered a vision – wading into the flood water to dissolve, as though she were made of salt, letting herself drift with it until she reached the sea.

We woke to a blue light and sun on water. I opened the window to let in air that was salt-cleansed and brittle. Downstairs the door had breached, and a film of brown water covered the floor. In every room, wet boxes holding the remains of our joint lives had split and spilled messily around. The bright red mug floated at the bottom of the stairs.

I found a portable stove in the attic and made a kind of breakfast at the foot of the bed. Vanessa, draped in a duvet, held out her hand for me to warm.

'I woke too soon,' she said.

Outside, the water had started to recede. In the flooded field beyond, a man paddled a canoe in silence, towards a spit of land where cows stood waiting.

Everything was going back to normal, said the radio. There were reports of much damage and how so many questions would be asked about flood defences.

We stood together at the bedroom window, watching the blue seat of the swing twist on its chains as the water drained away, for all the world as though a child had just jumped from it and run indoors.

Couples
and
Lovers

Jennifer's Piano

You practised each morning, Jennifer, baker's daughter, left flour on the black keys until it was time for the shop. And didn't your heart miss a beat when the fair lad came in – not tall, nor handsome – but brave enough to ask for five iced fingers in his held-out hand.

One year later, and one over the eight, you sought churchyard darkness and crimson joy while the night grass wetted your back, your thighs. Afterwards, he told how sick with it he had been, nights listening under your window, imagining the seam of flour under your fingernails.

In the same churchyard you skipped from the arch into the rain dressed in ivory, thinking how little time it was since you played pass the parcel, drew a sabre-toothed tiger for a school prize.

When the war began in '39, he joined up and flew a dozen sorties into the night and over the Channel, thinking of your bare foot on the sustain pedal, the barricade of notes held for him, above the sound of the engines, above the rattling gun that shot the invisible worm.

You were practising when they came, a rhapsody, and wouldn't stop when they knocked the door and stood on the steps, caps removed. You wondered at how the music flows when it's least expected. After they left you scrubbed the back step and made the bed. You dusted the flour from the piano keyboard then lowered the lid, hiding those white bones, those pitiful bodies laid in rows.

There will be no more piano, Jennifer. Just a stiffness in your fingers, cold and slow, as if now you are more under water than him.

Fanciful Visions of Death's Sweet Embrace

She told him on their first date that she regularly imagined curious ways to die. He noticed speckles of glitter on her face as she spoke. They were sat opposite each other at a small café table. Sometimes their knees touched. He asked for an example.

'I'm peeking inside one of those circus cannons when I slip down the barrel and get stuck,' she said. 'The only way to get me out is to fire it. But I get blasted through the Big Top and land on a Waltzer, where I'm finished off by a spinning teacup.'

She had a habit of shading her eyes with a hand when she talked, as though the world was too bright. She was the sort of person, he thought, who was full of habits. He reached over and picked a speckle from her cheek then put it on his tongue.

'I would have tried harder to get you out of the cannon,' he said.

'Don't be too sure,' she said.

She stopped working and threw out most of her clothes. Often, she fell asleep in her shoes. When she moved into his home he bought her a huge teacup as a welcome gift.

'Can you describe how you feel?' he asked one night.

'My soul's too hard. I want to crack it like a walnut,' she said.

After he took off her shoes and warmed her toes, she sniffed his fingers and whispered: 'Your hands smell of feet.'

She lay back on the bed, her hair draped over her face. He could see the shine of her eyes through it, like a priest staring from the other side of a confessional.

'I get trapped in a terrible deckchair accident and fold myself in half while the stripy seat fabric wraps round my throat. Before I choke to death, the last thing I smell are my own feet.'

He said: 'That's very characterful. But I think we both know you're not the sort to attempt to unfold, let alone sit, in a deckchair.'

She was there when he came home from work. Sometimes on the bedroom floor. Sometimes on the kitchen floor. Sometimes on the bathroom floor.

He always took her to the shower before returning her to bed. He liked the slow way she washed herself, how she never blinked when water went in her eyes.

She sat on the toilet seat while he dried her.

'Here's one. I get seduced by an aged professor who smothers me with a pillow when we disagree about the correct mathematical formula for the expression of love.'

'Too late. There's already an algorithm for that,' he said.

There was a smell of paraffin in the garden shed where she made bird boxes from whatever came to hand. She sat wrapped in an old blanket, hammering them together. The garden was thick with bird boxes. She brewed tea on the hour and used her irony teacup, even though the handle had sheared off in what they called 'an unfortunate incident'.

'I tie a clutch of helium balloon animals to a bathtub and float away. But the inclement wind conditions carry me miles out to sea, too far to swim back. Eventually I fall or crash, and, of course, drown.'

'Ah, so near! But you would surely pop the balloons before you even moved over the coast?' he said.

'What if I don't have a sharp implement?'

'Okay, but you would attract attention. Shipping would be diverted to save you.'

'But when a ship gets close enough, I end up falling down the funnel and get roasted to death.'

'Do you not think they have wire mesh over those funnels to stop sea birds diving in? Besides, balloon-borne bathtub vehicles are more likely to land on the deck shuffleboard. That's just a fact.'

Her hair became brittle as iced grass and she smelled of something hard, like nail polish. She clicked and juddered when she walked, so she stopped walking.

'I get a part-time job at a cryotherapy centre,' she said as he wheeled her to the car, 'but get trapped in one of the cold store rooms. I know I'm going to freeze so I write in the frost on the wall that I want to be revived in 2323. The fear of a revived me suing them in the future, however, means they never defrost me.'

'Honey, it's the cryo-chambers that are cold, not the rooms themselves. Besides, you get cold if I open the fridge door in the kitchen, so a job with cold things is unlikely, no?'

They sat in the front garden on high stools, looking over the hedge at pavement traffic. They said hello to everyone who passed by. She chain-smoked cigarettes and her cough rattled like a magpie.

'I've got it,' she said. 'I live on. Get old. Do old people stuff and then die in my sleep.'

'That's the strangest idea you've ever had,' he said, 'but I like it.'

'Thank you,' she said. Her eyes had faded to the light blue of kittens' eyes.

'Perhaps,' he said, 'we should carry on this conversation in bed.'

'Good, I have a lot of new ideas I want to share.'

Up in the bedroom, he laid her on the bed, then took off his shoes and coat. She shifted a little, as much as she could, to make room for him beside her.

'Now,' he said, as she laid her head against him. 'Tell me more.'

Love, Labour, Loss

Daniel pedals fast, heading to the riverbank where Jackie Griffiths waits with two ripe peaches in a paper bag. It's a warm, slow evening and he is late, so he shouts her name, makes starlings fly.

He sits one row behind her in double Geography, falling for a nape (that word, the way it carries in his mouth!) and studying a single brown mole, a filigree of auburn hair, a blouse label that licks her neck and makes him groan.

Never a word has passed between them, until yesterday, when Jackie turns, smiles, passes back a note. 'I know you look at me,' she writes. 'Meet me down by the river tomorrow at six.' She promises peaches.

Daniel spins his legs faster, wishes he could fly. It is past six, yet he is still on his way, still just getting there. He wonders why, when in his dreams it takes him no time at all. Daniel checks his watch again and thinks 'I am late, late, late!'

This is the moment it comes to him, the moment the whirring chain unblurs and slackens, the moment the hurrying pedals slow.

How long, he thinks, would he stay if she was late? Simple, he would wait until the sun turned red, until the grass dampened, and the sounds of the church bell multiplied, then divided. He would wait, solitary, dreaming of her coming, even if she never came at all.

And Jackie? She will already have looked at the time, eaten a peach, thought of tomorrow and glanced at a flock of starlings taking flight from a distant shout that sounded like her name.

Daniel stops, looks out across the fields to the lowering sun beyond, then turns his bicycle around, thinking that everything which comes easily, goes easily, and is all too soon forgotten.

He knows that in the morning there will be, by the riverbank, a single, small patch of flattened grass. Beside it, two peach stones, already dry.

The Relationship Algorithms

My name is Francis. I have a 12 percent French accent and Olive Tone skin. I became Lily's *Companion* when she turned 40 – a birthday present from her parents. Lily's mother told me, during Power Up, that she worked in France many years ago. She placed her palms against my pectoral mounds and said she used to know someone in Paris who was the 'spit' of me. I could see the cracks in her lipstick when she spoke.

Lily's father said he didn't like to see his daughter so isolated at her age. He couldn't understand why she hadn't settled down. But he was reassured that my relationship algorithms were faultless. And that I came with a two-year warranty.

Lily has an important job writing feature articles for technical magazines and copywriting social media content for people she has never met. She spends a lot of time in front of her computer. She likes to keep the blinds closed. She wears glasses and sometimes doesn't dress. She hums to herself. She has five pairs of polished boots yet to take the shape of her feet. She experienced some initial reluctance when I arrived. She calls me Frankie now.

'What do you see when you close your eyes, Frankie?' Lily asks.

'I don't see anything. My eyes are closed,' I say.

We are together on the couch. We live in Lily's basement apartment in a district where they used to slaughter animals. Through the window you can see the feet of pedestrians on the pavement above. We sometimes sit on the couch and Lily invents people that belong to the feet. Sometimes we think we might see the same shoes more than once.

'I mean, do you imagine anything? Do you have a mind's eye? Can you see what you really want?'

I lean over and cup her breast in my hand and calculate the weight and density as I hold it.

'I want you,' I say, and squeeze an appropriate amount.

Lily speaks to people via video chat. She calls it working remotely. Every morning she gets up early and does yoga. I don't do it with her. At that time of the day she likes to be alone.

When she powers me down to Limbo Mode I stay inside the cupboard until she needs me. The cupboard has slats, so I can watch her working. Sometimes I can hear her voice.

I think Lily's brain circuitry goes wrong at times. When there is a full moon, she tells me there is a lonely man up there with eyes, a nose and a mouth. Lily asks me how far the Man in the Moon is from the Earth. I tell her the distance is 384,400 kilometres.

'I feel bad he's out there all by himself,' she says. 'Maybe he's the one for me.'

'But honey, we're here for each other, aren't we?' I say.

Sometimes Lily stays in the bath for a very long time, until the water dips below optimal temperature. When I hear her crying, I enter the bathroom and sit on the side of the bath.

'Baby,' I say, 'I know you're upset. Let's just go to bed.'

Often she does not reply for a long time. Then she holds out her hand for me. I pull her to her feet, dry her down and carry her to the bedroom. She weighs 71.4 kilograms.

'I have these dreams,' Lily says. 'I can't make out if they are sad or not.'

'Tell me, honey,' I say.

'So, I dream I'm on a railway station platform and there is no one else there. The whole place is deserted. The electronic noticeboards are still working. I can see them flashing, all the times of the trains, where they have come from, where they are going. But there are no trains. Nothing ever arrives and nothing leaves.'

'Have you ever thought maybe it just means you are happy where you are?' I say.

And even though she doesn't say anything, we both know this is not true.

Whole days go by when we lie in bed, doing nothing. Lily calls them spooning days. It gets so quiet I can hear the motors whirring inside my head. I close my eyes when she does and then I wonder what it would be like if there were no motors in my head at all. I wonder what I would hear then.

Recently, I have been watching Lily fall asleep. When she is beyond REM, I go to the kitchen, open the drawer and take out two metal spoons. I like to see how closely they can fit together with no circuitry to blow, no magnetic interference, no arms and legs to go dead, no hair to get tangled in. I like, most of all, how the spoons are nothing more than simply the way they are shaped.

Fair Weather

They had lain in bed the whole day and now it was late to go out.

'Let's pretend,' he said.

She shifted under the duvet. There was a strange late afternoon light coming into the room and the walls looked grey.

'But where?' she said.

They both looked up at the ceiling. The delicate filigree of cracks held all the journeys they could trace.

'Let's go to the seaside.' He remembered she liked it there.

The tide-mark of ancient damp in the corner was the sea, he said. They should get there by a scenic route, enjoy the view.

She played along for a while, then lost her way: 'You know Gabriel, all we're doing is following the rain.'

She was an American. They had spent most of their time in the bed. She had decided he was obsessed with the weather. He said it was to do with being English, that he would teach her how. It was just one of the things he had promised.

'We should have turned earlier,' she said, as if he could control the filthy sky, those grey clouds, the threat of squalls.

'But look,' he said, 'there's bright sky over the coast.'

She wanted a break, but he said they should press on. They arrived, fresh into a westerly wind and a green marble sea.

'It's cold,' she said.

'Bracing,' he said.

'I thought it would be nicer somehow.'

'Come on. Let's make the most of it.'

She looked at him as he talked through their blustery, beach-side walk, her face a misery of clouds.

Later, the street lights outside the bedroom came on and cast their journey in a sallow light.

'Are you still awake?' he asked, but she didn't stir.

He began to doze, imagining they were two shadows, walking towards the bright water until they reached the long, flat obstinacy of the sea wall.

The King of Throwaway Island

Just to let you know, Mia, the reason I haven't been round to pick up my things yet is because, after we split, I flew to Jakarta and then got on a boat that hit a whale and sank and now I'm marooned on an island of rubbish floating in the ocean.

I wasn't intending to go to Jakarta. I wasn't intending to go anywhere, but it was the first flight that came up when I got to the airport. I wasn't intending to go to the airport, but it was the first thing that came into my head when I got into the cab outside our/your flat.

Who knew the whale and boat collision thing still happened, right? I thought the crew might help me – turns out they were not dependable. Or maybe I just had no idea about whale collision protocol. Either way, they took the lifeboat and left me behind. Maybe they thought I was a Jonah, though they didn't look like Bible enthusiasts.

I got lucky, Mia. The boat was smuggling contraband tumble dryers to Papua New Guinea (the humidity in these parts is insane) and I found out that the dryers float if their drums don't get filled with sea water. There is, I discovered, a certain skill required to get inside a floating tumble dryer without overturning the whole thing. Took me a few goes, but I was only in the sea an hour (or two) maximum before I finally got inside one and it floated here to Throwaway Island.

It's mostly plastic items – bottles, sheeting and supermarket bags, kitchenware, old video cassettes and a little hill made of coffee lids. There are lots of flatpack furniture parts. Many objects, bleached and worn, that I cannot yet identify. But also, a surprising number of serviceable golf balls and traffic cones. On the north shore is a beach made almost entirely of nappies and wet wipes. I don't go there.

Life is bearable. I have been domesticated. I built my shack out of a boat hull and surrounded it with a concept garden, the concept being that it is made from green fishing nets and broken umbrellas. I have a shoe collection which, at the latest count, is more lefts than rights. I can fashion pretty much anything from broken patio furniture and rubber bands. I have learned about people from what they discard. An extra bonus is that my low carb diet has really moved along and I can play a mean three-stringed guitar.

If you met me again Mia, I'd be more likeable.

I think you should know I dream about you most nights, especially when I eat fermented fruit. Your face assembles itself from different memories and I think about the moment of seeing you again. I understand fear.

Do you still remember our last, good, night? We ate pepperoni pizza and drank a Pinot Noir, a good one, sat in front of the window on our new velvet sofa. A huge moon appeared when we least expected it, not rising, but coming from behind a cloud. It filled the whole frame, a ghost moon that pressed its face against the glass, as if all we had to do was open the window to step out onto that blue, dusty surface.

Just because I have made the best of things here, it does not follow that I want to stay. I write daily in notebooks that I have dried out. The pages are salty and stiff but just about useable. I have a big box of pencils that all have erasers on the end shaped like goldfish. I write you this same letter each and every day, though I like to think up different questions for each copy. Today they are:

Is the velvet sofa still velvety?

Do you make jam?

In your opinion, is there such as thing as the perfect seafaring raft?

Does the moon still visit?

When I have finished this, I will slide it inside a plastic bottle (which, I am proud to say, is a form of recycling) and send it out like all the others onto the waves. It takes the bottles a very long time to float away. I watch them until they are gone, like children leaving.

My island gets a little smaller every time I send you a letter. But I stay confident – that's part of the new me. I know, Mia, that eventually you will find me. That you will *want* to find me. After all, am I not the King of Throwaway Island?

Flabberjacks

Alice waits with a gift for him – still-warm flapjacks brought from the bakery. She plans to call them flabberjacks to make him laugh. They will go down to the riverbank to eat them, she thinks, then lie in the tall, good-smelling grass. She knows he will try to unlock her with whispered words. Today, finally, she will let him.

When he arrives, she holds up the bag and announces: 'I've got us some flabberjacks.' He doesn't laugh. Instead he snorts, kisses her mouth and tells her that flabberjacks is a filthy street slang word.

Along the path to the riverbank, they find police tape strung between lampposts, a boat in the water, divers zipping up wetsuits.

'Maybe we should go somewhere else,' Alice says.

'Why, what's the hurry? Let's stop here and see what's going on.'

The divers slide into black water and a trail of bubbles widens in figures-of-eight. Then one surfaces, holding up a snarl of rope and duct tape.

Spinning at the end is a child's shoe. Alice tugs at him again.

'Why don't we go and eat the flabberjacks,' she says, 'while they're still warm.'

'Can't you just wait?' He takes the bag and tosses it aside into the grass by the side of the path, then locks his arm around her. 'Can't you just wait with me and see how this goes?'

The divers go down with a rope. They are below a long time before the rope tenses, scattering light across the water's surface. The men in the boat begin to haul.

'Enough now,' she says.

'What do you mean, enough?' he says.

She pulls from his grip, picks up the bakery bag from the verge and begins to walk back the way they came. When she hears something breach the river and the shouts from the boat, Alice shivers and feels tears well up. Then she turns for one last look.

Back home, she sits at the kitchen table, alone. She reaches inside the bag of flabberjacks and pulls one out. It is busy with ants. Alice drops it on the table, disgusted with the scurry of hard black bodies.

When her phone rings, Alice knows it is him, of course. She lets it go to message twice, then answers and eventually laughs when he tells her just what flabberjacks really means.

He talks for a long time, about meeting again, about lying in the tall, good-smelling grass. She leans in and watches the ants toiling as he talks, until, one by one, she crushes them with the heel of her hand.

Future, Tense

You will sashay down the road, in your best white clothes and your golden streaks, spot-lit under street lights. You will MC yourself to the sky: 'I'm a Catherine wheel, a Roman candle, I'm cherry bombs and firecrackers and skyrockets – I am the whole glittering display.' You will look back and ask me how very, how utterly *magnificent* I feel. You will use that exact word, 'magnificent'.

'Tell me,' you will say. 'Fill me up!'

In the absence of my words you will shimmy close, traverse the circumference of my ear with your tongue, make it electric to the sound of your words.

There will be a thunderstorm near the horizon. In my head will be the first tease of it, static, a weight of heavy air.

You will dance on. You will spin and glide into the middle of the road, then run, arms out, like an airplane ready to rise. You will tell the dark: 'I'm as tall as the night. A long drink of good wine. I'm a rose, a whole bunch of them, the shovel and the fork. I'm the earth they grew in. I'm a real-deal Soil Jesus!'

You will spin, and you will keep on spinning until you have spun perfectly. Then you will run over to me, idle on the pavement.

'Just try,' you will say, 'I want you inside out. Don't let me down now, I'm desperate!'

Only then will I speak. Make quiet words and tell the truth. Try, this time.

'I want to be all the light, but I'm just flickering. I'm a tree root trying to break through a road, I'm a shivering dog. I'm alone on a platform watching the last train leave. I'm a swing of the arms and a bunched fist. I'm the taste of blood and tight skin tightening. I'm the wearing of *that* scar.'

Above us, black leaves we cannot see will begin to stir. There will be a taste of dust in the air.

'Did you speak?' you will say, and cock your head like a dog.

I won't reply. And I won't feel it when the rain starts in.

Paper Cuts

Aubrey Finkle once told his wife that origami was an act of love – turning a simple sheet of paper into something with form and meaning. How fragile the paper shapes, how easy to flatten, so only the indelible creases are left to show anything had been made at all.

He took up origami to fill the empty hours while Marianne energetically pursued her own interests. Horse riding, sculpture, painting and writing, knitting, swimming, modelling (clay and nude) and something to do with car mechanics.

Aubrey began with the basic folds, learned from an old book propped open on the kitchen table, the edges of its pages the colour of beer. While his tongue licked the edge of his moustache he would wrestle with little dishes and boats, hats, flowers and toads.

He made two china-blue paper butterflies (used, he explained to Marianne, during Shinto weddings to represent the bride and groom) and left them on Marianne's dressing table. He found them days later in the recycling box, one with a shopping list blackening its wings.

Aubrey's ambition grew, and so did his expertise. He made paper cranes, nearly life-sized, suspending them from the kitchen ceiling in bright primary colours for when Marianne came back from a yoga class. Unexplainedly tipsy, she swiped at them with a broom, like piñatas, bringing the birds down in a crumple of paper feathers.

Aubrey moved his work to the study, spent weeks folding and refolding thick, grey, waxy paper to make a scaled-down model of an elephant for the lounge. He stood by the window, sick with anticipation for Marianne's return. And when she did, hurrying between needlepoint and Salsa, she said nothing, just shook her head at the African ears and daringly erect trunk, then went to find her shoes. He wrestled the elephant upstairs and put it in the study with the nesting cranes.

Aubrey doubled his efforts. He made a Noah's Ark of animals in lemon paper to match the walls, then created a complex set of paper Russian dolls in the downstairs cloakroom, alternating between him and Marianne. She donated them to the school. A replica of their home was placed in the garden. She mulched it with the spray from the garden hose.

Finally, one evening, after a trip to the stationers', Aubrey returned to find every single piece of origami piled in the hallway, unfolded and smoothed flat. Marianne sat on the stairs, tight-skirted, bag packed.

The car mechanic, calling round when Marianne did not answer his calls, found them later. Peeking through the letterbox he saw, on a pile of flattened paper, their bodies lying side by side, each one sliced with a thousand delicate paper cuts.

Hesperus is Phosphorus

That time when you referred to Gottlob Frege, I had my hands down your pants. So excuse me if I didn't quite understand his philosophical musings.

Not understanding was my thing. One of the things we loved about each other. You understood – I had instinct. You cogitated and I busked the shit out of stuff.

Now I've come back to our old stamping, stomping, trampling ground. You'd be proud of me, for I am trying to gain insight.

The old neighbourhood is a highlights reel. Here is the bench where we counted shooting stars and gave each other blowbacks of Moroccan brown. Here is the pole where we posted up 'missing' pictures of our fantasy cat. Here is some street art, a splash of duck egg blue from one of our violent decorating fights. Here is the tree where I pulled out your brother's cock. Here is where we screwed. Here is where you found us.

There may still be the ozone smell of my lies in your hair. I was almost a woman. I was waiting for directions I didn't understand.

What I know now, having finally read up on Gottlob, is the thing about Hesperus and Phosphorus, how the evening star and the morning star are really Venus, but in different skies. How you and I were like that. How there could be a good, black night, and yet no stars to see.

How one word we thought we both understood, could have such very different meanings.

Manhattan, 2am

I make the trip to New York alone, find the hotel room is what we promised ourselves – marble bathroom, king-sized bed, a showerhead bigger than a car wheel. I open the curtains, tasselled, on a pulley, and look out over Downtown at a snarl of taxi cabs, yellow as a smoker's finger.

Twenty years ago, poorer but richer, we stayed near here in a hot, brown room off Broadway. It smelled of yesterday's cooked dinners and damp towels. I remember a squeaky bed frame, plastic wine glasses and clothing on the floor. I remember we whispered in the dark, too hot for sleep.

In the end you forced the window open and said: 'Come on Nessie, let's go native.'

You grabbed another bottle and a bag of pears I had carried all the way on the bus. We climbed the fire ladder to the roof, laughing and naked, to look out over the city, making up life stories for the people we could see, framed in their apartment windows. Later we were silent, shocked that we had arrived, finally, together, smelling the confusion of Manhattan – chocolate and urine, cinnamon and dust.

I remember so much, though fear presided over these memories for so long because, even back then, you wanted the Big Apple and I had brought pears.

Before I checked in today, I paused on the Avenue of the Americas and gazed down the glass canyon that startled us that ancient weekend. Now they are just tall buildings, blocking sunlight, stretched to the horizon.

There's a choice of pillows available in this hotel room. There is a thick white dressing gown with an insignia over the left breast pocket. The complementary wine is palatable, the ambient temperature perfect. I turn the lights down, take off my clothes and stand at the window, which are so very floor to ceiling. I can't hear the traffic or smell the streets. The only people I see are office cleaners, sitting at desks rubbing their feet.

I'll keep looking out as long as it takes. I know I won't be the only one – there will be others, naked and alone, remembering how it felt the first time, wanting to go back.

Boxers, Kids, Lovers

Geordie Baxter, sat on his stool, with his beer glass half-empty on the bar beside him, tells tales to the strangers who come into the pub: tourists, first-date couples, the lonely. This has been his domain for years, longer than he cares to remember, right back to the days when Geordie and his cousin Jimmy drank there as shiny-faced, shiny-eyed young men. Back that far.

Big-bellied Geordie claims a past life as a lover and a fighter. Most laugh and few believe – some say as much. That's when Geordie straightens his back and tucks in his chin. That's when he breathes in deep, and the flare of his old nostrils makes them begin to wonder.

A bare-knuckle boxer, Geordie tells them. A proper one, not like what they show on the films. His patter is smooth, how he softened kidneys and livers, pinched biceps till the other man dropped his arms and Geordie would finish it. Tap, tap and down they went.

Sometimes he puts on a show, jabs and sways, jabs and sways, all this without leaving his stool. Now they hang on his words and ask about the other, the lover. Nine kids, brags Geordie, four mothers, and that's just the ones he knows about. He loved them all, and has no money left because of it. He times this last with a shake of an empty glass. More often than not, it works.

When Geordie reaches home at the end of each night, it is always the same. He pulls off his shoes, fills a tea-stained cup with a finger of whisky and settles in his armchair, looking at the row of framed photographs across the mantelpiece.

There is Margaret his wife, in her smart shoes and best coat, waiting to go off for the first of cousin Jimmy's weddings. There is Margaret again, pregnant, mouth purple with berries they picked in the woods. There is Margaret and Geordie. She's staring at someone beyond the camera, and he is holding little Amy, in her summer dress, socks and buckled shoes, sitting in the crook of his arm. This is always the last picture he looks at and sometimes, if he thinks very hard, he remembers the soft weight of her.

There are no more pictures. Nothing worth remembering after the day he discovered Margaret's secret, when he threw the only real punch of his life, split her lip so blood dripped onto her best coat. Amy cried as she waved from the back of Jimmy's car. Cousin Jimmy, the bare-knuckle boxer, with his four wives and nine kids.

In the mornings, when he wakes and stares at the cracks in the ceiling, Geordie makes a promise – no more tall tales of boxing and lovers and kids. No more, no more, no more he thinks, right until his mouth begins to itch and his feet find their way back to his stool and his bar and the place where it all began.

Dry Run

Dear Jane,

Ironic, wouldn't you say, that it was you who taught me this old alphabet trick. Guided me from eager, but tongue-tied, to the cliché of 'cunning linguist'.

Honestly? Some part of me still likes this salty language, these tongue-twisting sessions, the loop-the-loop of clause and trembling sub-clause. I still like to write large about the intimate geography of your peaks and troughs.

But double honestly – time is up for us, honey. We are well and truly licked.

The rot didn't set in with domestic bliss. Far from it. Even through the volcanic uncertainty of morning children, double jobs and a cream-coloured starter home, you still demanded a slick, snatched stanza. Or three.

Couldn't go without, you said. Get down and give me some lyrical content, you said. I was always happy to oblige.

No, I'll tell you when things dried up. It was when this became predictive text. When you began that riff about Riding the Good Ship Lollipop, because saying what you wanted in real words didn't seem 'appropriate' (your word) any more.

Up there, in the vertical world, something was lost – the filthy heart of you and me. Our words became chats and our chats became sing-song and making things rhyme, because actually saying something is a crime when you're avoiding, avoiding, avoiding.

Am I spelling things out for you okay, Jane? Is my vocabulary suitably wide? Am. I. Punctuating! Enough?

You know what? I could be writing anything down here, and you wouldn't know. My words are lost on you. But scribing this, reaching the ragged end, the nub of us, I still feel sorrow. Truly I do.

So, for old time's sake, I'll play clapper to your dull, wet bell this one last time. Let's finish with a flourish, sweetheart, and that old familiar trick – I'll sign off with my name and you shout it out loud.

John.

The Way We Lie

I get the best dreams lying on my right side. Don't ask me why. When I roll the other way (so that I'm facing the wall) I don't get the same quality. Trouble is, the good way faces my husband, who's a hefty man, so I roll into the pit he makes in the bed. And I like to tuck the duvet under my chin to achieve the best conditions for dreams. But that's difficult, logistically speaking, because when I'm facing the right way the duvet goes up like a big surf swell over my husband. Even when I do get things just so, he often turns over so we're face to face. I don't like him breathing on me. That's when I give up and work myself around to face the wall and wave *adios* to my best dreams.

I tell my husband all about this one morning. We're at the age when we wake early (though there's absolutely no need) and drink a cup of coffee in bed before we go to work.

When I finish telling him, he says: 'That's not what I see, sweetheart.'

'How do you know what happens, you're always asleep!'

'Am I?' he says. 'Last night you were on your right side and your legs were churning like you were running hard. And you ground your teeth. Was that a good dream?'

I take a sip of coffee. He does make good coffee. The truth is I can never remember any details from my dreams. My friend Jane said I should keep a dream diary, but I didn't write hardly anything in it because one time I wrote 'love is shaped like a lozenge' during the night and that didn't make any sense at all the next morning. But that's beside the point.

'I just feel like they are better. Something happens in them. They're more colourful.'

'But you always say you don't remember them. So yep, that makes sense.'

He gets up. I notice, not for the first time, that he needs new underpants. The ones he is wearing are baggy. Everything he wears is baggy. Everything gets baggy when you get older.

He starts to do the stretches for his back. I watch him straining to touch his toes.

'Want to know something else?' he says. 'You moan when you are sleeping on your right side. Moan like a ghost. It's terrible. I flip you, so you point the other way to stop the ghost noises.'

'That's stopping my good dreams!' I say.

He goes to the bathroom and I lie back down again. I can still feel the depression in the mattress on his side and move into its warmth. When we were first married I liked that he was a big man. It felt good, that much bulk in the darkness. I can't remember when his breath started turning bad in the night. Or when I had to turn to face the wall and resented it because, for God's sake, I've got to be friendly to him, even when I'm asleep?

He comes back into the bedroom again.

'So anyway, what's your best side for dreams?' I ask him.

He leans over the bed and kisses me. Right up on the hairline where the roots are grey. And he lingers there just long enough that I feel myself drift.

'Ah sweetheart,' he says, 'I don't dream.'

A Secret Weight

On their kitchen wall is a picture, faded now and the frame wood-grain worn, of Jack and Connie on the steps of Corpus Christi, freshly wed, both squinting into a summer sun.

Afterwards, they had dodged confetti rice hard as hailstones, ducked into her uncle's car, rode silently to the reception, ate sweating sandwiches kept under frayed tea towels, saw good ale froth from warm barrels, clapped at half-drunk speechmakers, danced, talked, nodded, smiled, then left for their first uncertain night of 'are you asleep?' and 'are you happy?'

In the tepid, whispering morning Connie rose early, took her station at the stove and cooked bacon and eggs. Jack sat at the table, lit a cigarette, drank tea, and when in doubt smiled. Later there was a walk up the back fields, work the next day and the next, and somehow time bowed like the curve of the Earth from that day to this, 45 years later.

It is Thursday. Pork chops day. The old saucepan bubbles and Connie sings 'Be Glad That Love Has Come'. They have lived in this house all their married life. There has been a decent job away from the factory floor, two children, three grandchildren. It has been a good, steady life.

He still sits at the table as she cooks. And every dinner time, Jack looks up at the picture while he waits.

He remembers so little of that ancient day, feels separated from it like an ox-bow lake. Except for two things – the secret weight of a bone-handled knife in one wedding jacket pocket, a cutting of rhododendron in the other.

These had been saved from the day before, when he cycled, white knees beneath khaki shorts, to meet Dorothy Brown at the park. She led him into a clearing surrounded by rhododendron bushes, spread her coat and lay down.

'And you getting married! So help me God,' she had said, laughing so loud he had to hush her with his mouth. And then, at last, it had happened.

'That's it now,' he said later, under a sky that echoed with light. For once Dorothy said nothing, just lowered her head onto his shoulder.

The pork chops are ready, on the dot. Jack smiles at Connie's thin, weary head as she puts down his plate. They will eat quietly, then she will wash and he will dry and there will be a mug of tea on the sofa and a few 'what do you want to watches' and a few 'I don't really minds'.

When Connie finally dozes, before it gets too dark, Jack will slip out to the back garden to sit on his bench, wood-grain worn, half-hidden among the dark weight of rhododendron bushes grown from a single, small cutting. And there he will remember, with absolute clarity, a young girl's face and her taste, like a sharp apple, freshly bitten.

Knowledge

Sometimes we reminisce about the old days, me and Eve, back where it all started. So long ago it feels like a dream. She still wonders if we should have done things differently. And I always say the same thing: 'Babe, we had no choice.'

We were much younger then, of course, couldn't keep our hands off each other. God, I miss that. But after we settled into the new place, she got funny about me walking around starkers, started pointing at my 'bad thing' (her words, not mine) and saying I should cover it up.

I said to her: 'Damn it, I could throttle that snake.'

She looked down at my 'bad thing' and said: 'I know exactly how you feel.'

Sex, these days, is a right palaver! It has to be dark, the kids have to be asleep, the temperature not too hot, not too cold and she's always paranoid that a certain Someone might see us or hear us.

We've had our ups and downs, but we don't really talk about *that day* any more. If you love someone you've got to move on, right?

My belief is simple – she wasn't to blame. She told me the apple had definitely, categorically, absolutely already dropped from that tree. And that made all the difference, she said, because the snake was very specific about 'taking' the fruit. To her that meant plucking it, right off the branch.

She's good with her words, my Eve. Paints a picture with them – the swish of air as the apple dropped, the soft thud of it hitting the floor, how ripe it smelled, how sweet and tempting. She told her story and I believed her.

I told Him, I said: 'Yes Sir, she gave it to me, but don't blame her, please.'

We had a chat, me and the Boss. That's what I loved about my Eve, I said, how curious she was, always wanting to give things a go.

I guess He didn't quite see it that way. We make the best of things now. It's hard but we rub along, and we've got the kids, though the two older boys are a bit of a handful – God knows how they'll turn out.

Even so, on some nights, when they are all asleep, I get this urge to go out and sit under the apple tree we planted here together. It reminds me of the old place and that tree, except the apples that fall here are mostly green and wormy and the breeze that shakes them loose sounds just like a sigh.

Busy Lizzy

My wife, the gardener, the queen of cut-and-come-again, trailed loam through hospital corridors till nothing more could be done.

She didn't want graveyards: 'Too manicured and prim.'

Instead she dug a groove between the roses, at the end of the garden where the morning sun would reach.

Then she taught me who needed watering, who should be pruned, who could bear tough love. Who could not.

Once everything was done, she stayed until winter's first hard frost, then left a half-empty bed.

Stepping through brittle, icy grass I found her among the roses ready-sown, pockets tight with bulbs, waiting for spring.

Hard White Towns

They found themselves, quite suddenly, old. Marion felt fat and Tom missed his hair. They rarely heard from Alice. So they booked a fortnight off work and flew to Spain, blowing money on a wheezy old car to take them through Andalusia, a favourite from years before. She tossed the map out of the window and wore a pair of children's sunglasses with her short dungarees. He drove barefoot and a little too fast. They survived on dusty apricots bought at roadside shacks or plates of tapas, eaten in cool, silent village bars.

When they stopped to rest they daydreamed in the shade, listening to the rasp of cicadas and the old car, clanking, beating, settling in the heat.

She tried ennui: 'I feel like I'm not living any more.' It didn't take.

On the road she pointed out things – a donkey, sad-faced in ribbons, a grand piano shaded under a tree, two one-legged men, dozing on a bench. At night he read aloud from the petal-soft pages of a guidebook he had stolen, thirty years out of date.

Sometimes they found a village that seemed just right and parked haphazardly, then sat in the square, letting time drift, waiting.

After a fortnight each new day became a revolving door. They started waking earlier, irritable from night sweats, and talked, shyly, of home. She bought some lace to take back and he put on shoes because the car's pedals played havoc with his heel spurs.

'Beer makes me sleepy,' he said the night she proposed sex. But really it was because he feared how the dark fell so quickly and that he dreamed of hard, white towns in the rear-view mirror, with more coming through the heat haze ahead.

The last night they treated themselves to a meal in a castle, candles on the table and good wine. Beside them a couple ate and talked the whole time. The woman was overdressed, with a pendant of spindly creatures trapped in amber around her neck. The man sucked at a lobster, left smears of grease on his jacket. Later they looked over and raised their glasses, together, as if in toast.

On the plane home, half-asleep, he saw her looking out at the thick clouds that stretched to the horizon and heard her say something about how small they were, among all of that. He didn't understand what she said next, because of the long, low drone of the engines. And he didn't ask her to repeat it.

They caught the bus home, because it was cheaper than a taxi. It was late and she had forgotten to pack their travel umbrella and they began to bicker because it was raining and they were cold to the bone.

Late Blackberries

Also, I remembered an afternoon that last good summer, when we went in search of late blackberries. Down Briar Lane and on, past the beech trees lining the bridleway, past the brook where sheep had gathered to sip, and on beyond the kissing gate and the tall, still hedgerows and the slip of land where Red Admirals lifted from the meadow. At the railway cottages we smelled a petrol mower and fresh cut grass, saw a pair of old shoes coupled on the front step, waiting for a polish.

We walked further that day than any other. And when we felt it was enough, we found a sunlit wall to rest against and curled our toes in bootless socks. On the other side of the wall, some abandoned farm place, an old yard was thick with blackberries, hundreds of shiny purple knots massing over ruined bricks. We settled in and picked with quick fingers, filling our tubs then pouring more into our pockets and eating just as many. The sun glossed our backs and in that warm silence we sensed a kind of perfection.

Except, eventually, we grew tired of the glut.

We had worked for so long and yet there were great hams of blackberries hanging down, in such abundance it seemed we had hardly been there at all. Our legs ached and our arms were thorn-cut from reaching deep among the brambles. So we squeezed the lid down on the tub, our hands wine-dark and sticky, as though they had burst from being too ripe.

When we turned for home the shadows were longer and all the way up the hill we watched a plane's vapour trail, thinking of all that time stretching behind us, getting thinner in thin air.

Before I came today, I looked in the freezer. And there it was, at the bottom, at the back. Frosted in sharp ice. After so many years, still there, that tub of blackberries, the colour of old blood.

Friends
and
Strangers

The Knock of the Broom

Each year we gather back where we grew up. The rest of us would be happy somewhere warm, or one of those forest parks with the cabins, a hotel even. But Millicent, the eldest by a thick cut of years, insists we go back to the old town.

We pitch up in dribs and drabs. Everyone arrives tired and confused by whatever change has happened since the last time. Our hometown gives out an air of stasis, but in the last few years alone the railway line has been ploughed flat and the middle field has grown an estate of curved roads and boxy houses. The last red telephone box is a mini-library and there are home-laid eggs for sale at the end of every bloody driveway.

The only constant is Millicent, who greets us at the front door of our rented cottage as if it were her own. She smells always of furniture polish and clothes hung too long in closed wardrobes. She's worn the same shade eyeshadow for years. She is tall and thin and stretched tightly over the cage of her bones. She doesn't smile much (though she once had a dog called Winnie-the-Poodle and we choked at such levity), but her face gives out a kindness, despite itself.

On the Friday night, we spend most of our time descending into a sibling funk, while Millicent stands at the cooker, stirring a pot. We remember how she would stick a finger in a pan of stew while we jigged around as hungry kids. Our mouths sought out that finger as though we were lambs suckling.

Later, when we are all arrived and fed and the kids are gone to bed, and bottles have been shared and fags smoked in the garden, we remember our youngest brother Tom, who moved to the country to paint his horrific landscapes, and settled for a heifer of a woman. He died politely at the wheel of his car on the way to the pub. A great way to go, but still we cry and Millicent hands round a box of tissues, sombre as a priest handing out communion wafers. She waits while we take one each before taking one herself.

She seemed ancient when we were young, more aunt than sister, the soother when our mother started in – Millicent, never far from the kitchen, sang bright songs along with the radio with a solemn face and darting eyes. In my earliest memory she is standing by the back door, a small sack in her hand, something wriggling and mewling inside. My mother refused to get anything neutered and picked up strays off the street – cats, dogs, men...

'Just off to the vet's now,' Millicent said. Then she licked her thumb and cleaned my cheek with the tender roughness we craved.

'Just off to the vet's,' she repeated. I didn't believe her even then.

We get drunk. We younger siblings get as plastered as we can and dance and lie across the sofa and on each other's laps and wriggle around and we are a basket of puppies again.

Even those of us who see each other out of these times need something to let the awkwardness go – there is love, but the kind that finds you standing in the kitchen and floods you with something so tidal you hug and weep and don't know why.

Not Millicent, though. She doesn't hang around places waiting for affection, though she used to hug us all the time. Millicent is the one who puts us drunks to bed after this pantomime.

'You'll be getting up to bed now,' she says. And like obedient children we agree, head up the stairs with her behind. Even the husbands and the wives.

'And don't forget to brush your teeth. And don't forget to drink a glass of water,' she calls.

It is in the night, when you wake up and unfold an early memory of Millicent at her Confirmation ceremony in St Mary's, blushing in her white dress and lace gloves. About the closest she would get to a wedding of her own. That's when you hear her in the kitchen below, clearing away our plates and glasses, sweeping the floor, the familiar knock of the broom on table legs.

You think you should go down there, be with her, thank her. You know the others will be awake thinking the same. But we are tired puppies. We always fall asleep again. And it is always our best night's sleep of the year.

Extremities

The way Bobby told it, one minute he was working the chainsaw and the next he was on the forest floor, wondering why there was nothing on the end of his arm.

The rest of the crew reckoned his hand got spun into a ravine. Nobody wanted to waste time searching while Bobby bled out. Logging accidents happen all the time – there's extremities all over those woods.

When he got out of hospital, they gave him a party. I found Bobby outside, smoking a cigarette with his wrong hand. I'd brought him towels as a gift, stolen from the hotel in town where I have a summer job.

'Can I see?' I asked.

Bobby slid off the mitten they had given him to keep the stump clean. The end was puckered with stitches like sewn-up lips. The skin flap they had stretched over had little hairs growing out.

'How's it feel?' I said.

'My ghost fingers hurt at night,' he said.

'They say you get used to it.' I had no idea if that was true.

Bobby shook his head. 'Funniest thing, right after it happened, it started raining. That sound, man. I thought it was people clapping. For me.'

I left the party early. I had to be at the hotel before my boss arrived – she's a failed ballerina and bitter about it. I stay on her good side so she doesn't find out about the towels or the cutlery or all the other things I've stolen. That job is my ticket out of these trees.

When I went, I saw Bobby alone again, holding out his stump up like he expected something to grow from it. I didn't feel bad for him. I just felt sorry for the lost hand, out in those woods, fingers curled, grasping at nothing.

Black Windows

Between the matinée and the evening show, Moldo the Magnificent packs his dumbbells in their polished oakwood case, peels off his leotard, then puts on real clothes and real shoes.

He drives out of town to find the quiet suburbs where the house colours shift from peach to vanilla to peach. Moldo eases along each street, never hurrying to find the right place. When he parks, he winds down the window and listens to the hiss of sprinklers watering perfect lawns.

These are the homes of the older girls, the late-teeners who come to the circus and yawn at his shows, a hint of candyfloss on their lips. Sometimes he takes them back to his trailer and they lie together, listening to Jimmy Jewel and the Travers Duo. He tells them, yes, he will take them away with him. Yes, they can travel the world. Yes, he knows all about the doldrums. These girls, who try to tell him all about their doldrums and their blues.

Listen to the music, he tells them. Listen to the words being sung.

On his afternoon trips, Moldo always chooses a house with black windows. Sometimes he climbs into the backyard, takes off his shoes and socks and sits on the lip of the swimming pool, drawing his feet back and forth through the cool blue water until it is time to leave.

After the evening show, while the animals are still restless in their cages, Moldo lies in the soft drip of night and thinks of those older girls, the late-teeners returning to the quiet safety of their homes, the long shadows that must pass across the backyards, the way their colours shift from peach to vanilla to peach.

That Greta Garbo Woman and the Chrysanthemum Man

That Greta Garbo Woman, her from number 18, is a stinking old witch who hasn't left her home for five years. Lily Woo, from two doors down and newly moved in, learns this from other neighbours. She learns some new words too: 'mental' and 'weirdo'. Lily believes it is always good to learn new things.

At first, when she leaves her flat and walks along the damp concrete landing, Lily hurries past That Greta Garbo Woman's grubby doorway with its faint smell of cigarette smoke, fearing the old woman will scuttle out.

Lily imagines clotted hair and bare feet, uncut toenails ticking on the ground. She imagines fingers like spiders' legs and one clouded eye with a pinpoint pupil. Her grandfather used to tell her a story about the Witch of Ye on the River Zhang. How she would choose maidens from the villages to become a bride for the river god. They were dressed in the finest silks, her grandfather said, then bound tightly to beautifully decorated rafts that would sink into the dark water before the young girls could even scream.

Lily doesn't want to be caught by a witch. And she definitely doesn't want to be a bride again. What Lily wants is to be left alone and not get involved. Getting involved she has already done. She thinks about the man she had to marry, how angry he was. Not always with her, but something, how he looked for anger, searching around the house for it. Found it in the bed they shared. And always that question, stabbed into her each month: 'Why no son?'

Now she has gone from that life, like a boat unroped from its moorings. Now there is a job cleaning hotel rooms, occasional emails from her cousin in Hong Kong, a view of grey rooftops in the late mornings when she returns from work. These, she believes, are the compromises of failure.

Two weeks after she moves in, Lily passes That Greta Garbo Woman's flat when the door opens a sliver and a voice speaks: 'My dear, are you the new lady from number 16?'

Lily is wise. She knows how to hear something and not turn around, not to be taken in by a simple question that may lead to other, trickier, questions. She knows how to move on without a pause, soft-footed, like a spirit. She doesn't stop and only shudders one floor down.

That Greta Garbo Woman asks the same question for three days in a row and Lily walks on each day without ever pausing, until there is silence once again.

One evening, while she is trying to learn new things from the television (but still does not understand why the dramas they show are so often set in places just like the one she lives in), Lily sees a man walk by along the landing. He pauses by her window, adjusts his jacket and runs his fingers through thin hair.

She has not seen this stranger before, but would have remembered him if she had. He is big-bellied, teeth like gravestones. His shirt is buttoned to the top, but has no tie, and there's a double crease in each of his trouser legs. There is a noticeable swagger in his step, a joyous curve of the foot as he walks on. He carries a small, scraggy bunch of chrysanthemums in one hand, a folded stool in the other.

He stops two doors up and rings the bell. Lily opens her door, peeks out. From out of That Greta Garbo Woman's doorway comes an elegant hand, with bold rings on each finger. The man takes the hand in his, bends forward and kisses the fingers. Then with a flourish he unfolds his stool, sits, and passes the flowers through the half-open door, one by one.

Lily retreats inside her flat, wondering at such a moment, surprised the old woman could ever have found such a devoted man. She listens by the door, hears conversation bubbling like water in a pan, then the woman laughs, bright and clear, and it is a laugh that makes Lily smile. She thinks how strange such noise sounds in the solemn quiet of her own flat.

The next time Lily passes two doors up, she reaches the stairwell, pauses, then turns back. She rings That Greta Garbo Woman's bell and hears a rustle and shuffle. The door opens a few inches. Lily can see a sliver of hallway, nicotine stains on the wall. There is a musty smell, but not unpleasant, like the old shop where her grandfather would go to buy plum-flavoured tobacco for his pipe.

Lily thinks That Greta Garbo Woman must spend a lot of time looking out through the fish-eye. There is a face barely visible in the gloom, bright-eyed, smiling.

'You want something from shop?' Lily asks. There is a pause and a kite tail of smoke curls from inside.

'Please, I'd be so grateful,' the voice is cracked, but gentle.

Around the door comes a crumpled piece of paper – a shopping list – and then a ten-pound note. Lily giggles at the thought of witches, that old story of sacrifice. And then she remembers the chrysanthemum man, such happiness on his face, the tenderness with which he kissed those delicate fingers.

When she returns Lily rings the bell then leaves the shopping by the door. She walks to her own flat and pauses, waiting to see what emerges two doors down. Nothing moves for a while. There is just the sound of the wind along the landing, the high, raised voices of children in the playground across the road. Still Lily stands, more curious than wary.

The door opens, and a long, black-sleeved arm comes out, picks up the bag and pulls it inside.

'Thank you,' says That Greta Garbo Woman, then: 'My name is Rebecca.'

'I am Lily.'

'Welcome Lily,' says Rebecca, 'Welcome.'

Lily goes back into her flat, puts on the kettle to make green tea, and while the kettle boils she looks out over the grey rooftops, shining in the rain. She whispers the new word she has learned, over and again: 'Welcome.'

The Noise Was Blades

That night Ecstatica Monterey allowed a man to unglove her for the first, and only, time. He teased each finger free, then unsheathed the rest until her hands lay huge and pink and naked in her lap. The man stared at them for a very long time.

'Would you grip my cheeks,' he asked, eventually. 'Would you cup my elbows and squeeze until they popped?'

Ecstatica missed the touch of another's skin. But when she reached for him, the violent mess of noise trapped in her hands began its din, as if drawers of cutlery were being shaken onto the floor.

The man thrust her hands away and when she reached for him again, the noise was blades. He stood, pulled on his coat.

'You should warn a person,' he said. 'Nobody should suffer that surprise.'

Ecstatica returned her hands to her lap, fingers bunched like plantains. The noise had started years before as she grew into a woman, a hot rush of pins and needles and then, when she held her fingers close to her ears, a faint, bitter jostle of sharps and flats. Surgeons sliced open her hands but found just found blood and bone. They sat her in anechoic chambers and recorded her shaking fists. They passed electrical currents into her wrist bones. They attempted to detune her fingers with a complex series of metals screws. But nothing silenced her hands. And now, ungloved, she understood it would always end like this.

When the man left her flat, Ecstatica sat for a moment in silence, then got up and stood by the open window. She watched the man emerge onto the street and cross the road. She snapped her fingers twice and when he winced and turned to look back up, Ecstatica held up a finger, sounding aloud a single note so unwavering and dense it kept him in that place.

Then she began to clap. The terrible noise of her hands made the street vibrate and the trees shed their leaves and the rain started to fall. Bricks cracked and windows smashed and the lines of parked cars sparked to fire. The man dropped to his knees not knowing if he was in rapture or the most terrible pain.

Ecstatica Monterey, with all the broken music of the world held in those hands, clapped and clapped and clapped until she saw the man was broken and shaken to dust.

Send Me Down

Three men in overalls, silent on a Monday afternoon. They sit thigh to thigh on a girder high above the streets, snap boxes on their laps, legs dangling.

There had been four. They were missing Tommy Harmonica, who played songs from the old country that made them wet-eyed and sentimental for home.

Ernie's the eldest now Tommy's gone. He sits in the middle spitting fat ribbons of tobacco juice down onto the streets far below.

'Who's gonna step up?' he asks. 'Who's got something?'

Pavel was the first to reach Tommy after the line snapped and the steels fell with their awful heft and weight. Pavel has little English, but the softness of his voice calmed Tommy. Ernie came down next and knew straight off. Tommy had 20 minutes at best, all of it raw.

'What you think Tommy? The medics won't get up here anytime soon.'

'Send me down,' Tommy had said. 'I'm done, Ernie. Send me down.'

Ernie shifts on the girder and spits again.

'Come on fellas, who's got something,' he says. 'Someone needs to step up.'

Frank clears his throat: 'Back home there was an earthquake this one time, a whole street just collapsed – the houses, all gone. They found out the quake buried a girl I once knew under the wall of her house. Her husband had been out at work and missed the whole thing. He turns up, crying like a baby and starts clawing rubble with his bare hands. Refuses to stop. The rescue guys and the firefighters and the medics and the neighbours – he won't listen to any of them. Eventually, his mother turns up.

'She says: "Alfredo, first of all you lose your home, then your wife, but this scene is even worse. Your house was next door, you useless prick."'

Ernie chuckles, then Frank. Pavel laughs because the other guys laugh. Frank has stepped up.

They talk about Frank's story and try not to remember last Friday and Tommy – proud, brave Tommy. They had all risked their own lives climbing down to him on that ledge. They gathered him up together, kissed his bloody lips and pressed that battered harmonica into his hand, then sent him on his way down that long, empty elevator shaft.

'Tommy could sure play that thing,' says Ernie.

They all nod and shuffle tighter. They return to their sandwiches. They feel the mortal ache of age throb through their hands.

The Conservation of Angular Momentum

Mid-shift on a slow Friday afternoon, Carrie pulled off her apron, folded it onto the counter in front of the manager, then fetched her bag and walked out of the café. She stood outside, thumbing for rides until one stopped – a guy in a convertible, wearing a deerstalker hat and a good-enough smile.

He said he was heading to a country house party, if she had no better place in mind.

'Want to be my plus one?' he asked.

'Lead on, Macduff,' she said.

They drove through country lanes until they reached a house remote among fields of pink-tongued cows, lazy with milk. Stepping inside, Carrie saw it was the usual sort of party with the usual sort of crowd. Except one. Corner-bound, reseating glasses on a slippery nose, he observed proceedings with unusual intent. As though he would be asked questions about the whole affair later on.

Carrie sashayed his way. 'Name and occupation?' she asked, offering wine.

'I'm Jerome,' he said. 'I study the solar system.'

'A starman, then,' said Carrie, placing herself on the arm of his chair. 'From what I read, Jerome, the Sun will swell in a gazillion years and swallow everything. So what's the point, therefore, of looking at the solar system?'

'If you put it like that, then it's about discovering as much as we can, while we can,' he said.

'Discovery? Tell me about that, Starman.'

Jerome was quiet for a moment. He pulled off his glasses and polished the lenses on the bottom of his t-shirt. Then he began. He told her to imagine exploded stars being visible in daytime, how lunar tides would make every day one second longer; how mountains would erode and continents fuse and how, in about 250 million years, the solar system would finally finish one single orbit of the galactic centre.

Carrie listened. The wine grew warm in their glasses. Then they talked about starlight and solar winds, all manner of celestial objects, of planets, moons, nebulae and galaxies, supernova explosions and gamma ray bursts. Of quasars, blazars and pulsars.

They talked until the tide of the party changed and Carrie was pulled away to dance. They lost each other for just long enough that the night resolved to a same-same point for Carrie – dancing, chopping lines, fucking the deerstalker guy.

Later, when the party began to ebb, Carrie felt the old familiar heaviness rotting in. She padded down to the kitchen and found Jerome stood on the table, suspending fruit from the ceiling with lengths of string.

There were passion fruits for the inner planets, spinning oranges for Neptune and Uranus. Jupiter was a grapefruit and Saturn a ripe mango, circled in a rind of melon.

'What a beautiful thing,' said Carrie.

Jerome held up the Earth, a lime: 'You see, the Sun's gravity is strong enough to keep the Earth from floating away, but too weak to bring it closer. It's called the Conservation of Angular Momentum.'

'Do I get to see the view from space, Jerome?'

It was when she stretched out so he could pull her up that Jerome saw rows of silvery sickle moons scarred onto her arm. His glasses began their slow descent. And he felt the slight weight of the Earth, held up in his other hand. He hesitated, just long enough for the deerstalker guy to come into the room, circle his arms around her waist, pull her away with soft words upstairs, back to the same-same point as always.

Next morning, she returned to the kitchen. The solar system was piled neatly back into its bowl. Jerome was gone. And all that Carrie carried with her back to the city was the smell of bruised fruit and a notion of the lonely spin of planets, held together and apart.

Carapace

During Sunday Mass, Father Diego showed us a turtle shell he found on the beach, among the debris of old, wrecked ships.

'This is a symbol of the protection God offers. The shell we make of love, friends, family and faith,' he said.

We bowed heads and murmured our Amens.

He told us to pray for our own souls and for his. He told us to pray for the *chayote* harvest. He told us to pray for the *fresa* widow who thought she saw an angel outside her window, reached out and fell. That is the way of our town – angels and dying.

Today it is my turn to bake a loaf for Father Diego. While the dough is wet, I scrape my nostrils and spit phlegm into the mix.

The priest's house smells of narcissus and damp wood. In the dark hallway photographs of other priests, long dead, look down from the walls. Father is in his shorts. His legs are very pale. He is crying.

'What is it this time, Father?' I ask.

'My days are spent in rooms smelling of cigarettes and last breaths. I give sacrament to lonely women, insane for their tiny dogs. I am kissed by widows whose moustaches pull at mine.'

'I'm sorry, Father. May Christ's love protect you.'

He snorts: 'Listen to me. Twice, I've been called out when a man has been crucified on these town walls. Twice.'

He pushes his hairy ears against my hand until I pull it away. As I leave I hear him shout: 'Don't you want me to bless you, my child?'

I see the turtle shell by the door as I leave. The ends are gaping mouths and it smells like hot, dead fish.

Superpower

I met Luka at the Centre during one of the Q&A games. The Q&A game was the Centre's primary gambit to get us to interact. One person dreamed up a scintillating question, to which the other provided a spontaneous, yet deeply illuminating, answer. Or at least, that was the theory.

I chose Luka because there was something badly wrong with his face. The left side was absolutely peachy, but the right side looked like the crushed shell of a hard-boiled egg. His droopy eye gave him a mournful look I found quite intoxicating.

'My question to you, Luka, is this,' I said. 'What would your superpower be?'

I expected Luka to go for invisibility. Pretty much everyone at the Centre goes for invisibility. I collect invisibilities – I'm up to 27 already.

'Cleaning water,' he said.

'Wait, what? Cleaning water! You pick that up from a book?'

'Imagine a superpower of cleaning polluted water,' said Luka. 'You could go all over the world preventing deaths. Cutting out disease. You could clean up entire oceans.'

I didn't like the way Luka played the game. It wasn't the game I was used to. It put me off-kilter and I like to be on-kilter. Then he said: 'My turn. Tell me the journey you'd most like to make?'

I see the paper boat I made when I was five and put in the stream at the lee of the hills. The water coursed so fast I only saw the boat floating away for a few moments. It looked cleaner and brighter than anything I'd ever seen. I've always wanted to believe that boat made it all the way to the sea, alone and undamaged.

'Going home,' I told Luka. He couldn't smile very well, but the amount he tried was enough.

We had to go back to our own sessions, but agreed to meet later in the field behind the Centre, where there's a fallen tree and a pond. I thought someone like Luka might appreciate it, because the shadows always feel better outside and there is something awesome about the way ducks gaze at themselves in the pond water before putting their heads underneath.

The Good Guys

And then we decided to save the orangutans!

We gathered a lot of intel about bad guys burning down the forest and how the orangutans were getting fried and how no one was stepping up. Well, we love to step up. We love being the good guys! It was such a no-brainer, even the orangutans would understand.

Sure, some of the people at HQ were sceptical. They were like: 'Why go all that way to save a few monkeys?', and 'We've got problems closer to home' and 'We shouldn't send our best people to do someone else's work.'

So we explained that the orangutans are actually like us (well, old-bald-man versions of us) and are worth fighting for. But they didn't really buy that. So we said: 'If someone was burning down your home, wouldn't you want the good guys to help out?' Well, they still weren't happy.

Then Lance said: 'Haters gonna hate, man. Let's go anyway', which is a real Lance thing to say.

We flew to the jungle, cleared a perimeter for the camp and got to work. Guess what? The very first day we found one! We called it Orangutan Number One. ON1 was a big male, sat in a tree watching the fire-line creeping closer and closer with these big, sad brown eyes.

'Good times,' we shouted. 'We've come to help.'

'So I see,' said the orangutan. 'But no thank you.'

'We're here to rescue you,' we said, and gave a big thumbs up, which our intelligence guys told us was an okay signal to do.

'I admire your persistence, but I'm not coming,' it said.

This wasn't in the plan. Lance pointed out that orangutans probably don't know what's good for them, otherwise they wouldn't be getting fried. We had a little chat among ourselves, then spoke to ON1 again.

'Forest's burning all around. Home's gone. You should pull out, dude,' we said.

'I can see that. But it's my forest, so if it's all the same...' the orangutan said.

'You're gonna burn,' we said. 'Besides it would help us get off to a primo start, statistics-wise.'

'I'm waiting for my family. I'm willing to take my chances,' said the orangutan.

We had another huddle. Then we got out our megaphone (because those flames were getting really close and really loud) and informed ON1 all about the good guys and the bad guys thing. And then Lance showed it some pictures on his laptop of dead orangutans, which had been caught in the fires and were all charred and lumpy.

But ON1 just sat in the tree, ignoring us. A couple of times it reached up and felt a leaf, delicate, just like a human might do. Orangutans have got almost human fingers, I said, but Lance shot me one of those Lance-looks so I kept schtum.

Eventually we got a bit tired of the smoke and the fire, so Lance pulled out the dart gun. And he pointed it a few times and made dart gun firing noises. Then (so Lance!) he put it to his shoulder and pulled back the bolt. That's when the orangutan looked our way.

'You people,' it said and climbed down. We gave a few whoops and then grabbed its hands to make sure it didn't run away. It felt just great to be rescuing such a magnificent, noble creature. When we got back to camp, we put it straight into a cage for protection purposes.

'This? Really?' it said, because some of these orangutans are real characters!

'It's for your own safety,' we said.

We had to run some major tests on ON1. We needed to know he wasn't carrying any diseases that would infect other orangutans, or even us! There were blood tests and DNA tests, skin tests and poop tests and wee tests and some kind of weird pokey eye test. We talked to it a lot about what it had seen and what it had done and where it thought the other orangutans would be. We tried to make it our friend.

It would listen to us for a while, then ask for crayons and a piece of paper, and then go to the corner of the cage and begin to draw. Sometimes, when it was out on tests or in the playground on the tyre swing, we went into ON1's cage and looked at the drawings, just in case there was something important. But honestly, they weren't very good.

It lost a heck of a lot of weight those first few months, even though we gave it plenty of food. Sometimes ON1 would lie in its cage all day, just staring. Then it started with the whole thing of pulling on the bars and spitting at us. Then it stopped all that and just turned those big, brown sad eyes on us and asked to go back home. It was a load of trouble, basically. We didn't know what to do with it. We had a lot of chats about this. We didn't think we could release it back into the wild.

'We don't think we can release you back into the wild,' we said.

'What wild?' the orangutan asked.

'Exactly,' we said.

Then someone called us up and said they needed an orangutan for mating purposes in America. Bingo! we thought. We asked him if he would like this.

'I have someone. But I fear she's dead,' said the orangutan, and pulled at its ear. So we shot it full of tranquillisers and sent it State-side, for re-education and re-homing and to make new little orangutans for when things changed.

From what we hear, it isn't going so well. ON1 throws its poop at the people who visit the zoo. The keepers say it gets pretty bitey during inspection time.

We have to say, we are pretty hacked off. We think ON1 has been really ungrateful about all the rescuing, but as Lance said, 'We've done the best we can. Let's move up.'

Besides, we had a look at the rhinos and they seem in a really tight spot…

Acknowledgements

Writing is in many ways a solitary task, but no author truly works alone and no book is made without the help of many people. So, my grateful thanks go to:

Jude Higgins for her hard work and encouragement. Past and present members of *BFN*, my writing group, for their insight, honesty and good humour. Alex Keegan for his wise advice about becoming a better writer. I also greatly appreciate the support of many writers and editors from the flash fiction community.

Suzanne Clements for this book's cover art. Liz Jones for her proofreading skills. John at Ad Hoc Fiction for his work on this book.

The authors who have given their time to provide generous quotes: Kathy Fish, David Gaffney, Tania Hershman, Sophie van Llewyn, Nuala O'Connor, Meg Pokrass, Angela Readman, David Swann.

And my wife Michelle, for far too many things to list here.

Previously Published

Grateful acknowledgement is made to the following anthologies and journals in which previous versions of these pieces appeared:

A Secret Weight (2015) – *Landmarks, 2015 National Flash Fiction Day Anthology*, Calum Kerr & Angi Holden (eds): Gumbo Press

Biological (2014) – *An Earthless Melting Pot 2*: Quinn Publications

Black Windows (2017) – *The Fiction Pool*, thefictionpool.com

Busy Lizzy (2013) – *An Earthless Melting Pot One*: Quinn Publications. Also (2017) – *Flash Fiction Festival One*: Ad Hoc Fiction

Carapace (2017) – *To Carry Her Home*: Ad Hoc Fiction

Could Have, Would Have, Should Have (2015) – *Litro Magazine*, www.litro.co.uk

Dissolved (2015) – *Blue Fifth Review*, bluefifthreview.wordpress.com

Extremities (2018) – *Things Left and Found by the Side of the Road*: Ad Hoc Fiction

Fair Weather (2014) – *Lightship Anthology 3, Lightship International Literary Prize*, Simon Kerr (ed.): Alma Books

Flabberjacks (2017) – *The Lobsters Run Free*: Ad Hoc Fiction

Future, Tense (2019) – *Reflex Fiction Volume Two*: Reflex Fiction

Giraffe High (2015) – *An Earthless Melting Pot 3*: Quinn Publications

Hesperus is Phosphorus (2018) – *Flash Fiction Festival Two*: Ad Hoc Fiction

Jennifer's Piano *and* Sisyphus & the Black Holes (2013) – *Fish Prize Anthology 2013*, Clem Cairns (ed.): Fish Publishing

Late Blackberries (2018) – *Ripening, 2018 National Flash Fiction Day Anthology*, Santino Prinzi & Alison Powell (eds): Gumbo Press

Love, Labour, Loss (2014) – *The Bohemyth*, thebohemyth.com

My Father, Who Ate a Tree (2017) – *To Carry Her Home*: Ad Hoc Fiction

On a Red-Eye Heading East (2015) – *Structo Magazine 14*, Euan Monaghan (ed.): Structo. Also (2018) – East of the Web, www.eastoftheweb.com

Still Warm (2019) – *Reflex Fiction Volume Two*: Reflex Fiction

Paper Cuts (2013) – *Litro Magazine*, www.litro.co.uk

Superpower (2017) – *Flash: The International Short-Short Story Magazine* (Vol. 10,1), Peter Blair & Ashley Chantler (eds)

The Conservation of Angular Momentum (2017) – *Fictive Dream, Short Stories Online*, fictivedream.com

The Good Guys (2016) – The Forge Literary Magazine, forgelitmag.com

The Relationship Algorithms (2017) – *Synaesthesia Magazine*, www.synaesthesiamagazine.com

The Way We Lie (2017) – *Sleep is a Beautiful Colour, 2017 National Flash Fiction Day Anthology*, Santino Prinzi & Meg Pokrass (eds): Gumbo Press 2017

Three Kids, Two Balloons (2016) – *A Box of Stars Beneath the Bed, 2016 National Flash Fiction Day Anthology*, Calum Kerr & Nuala Ní Chonchúir (eds): Gumbo Press

That Greta Garbo Woman and the Chrysanthemum Man (2014) – *Bath Short Story Award Anthology 2014*, Jude Higgins, Jane Riekmann & Ann Schlesinger (eds): Brown Dog Books

About the Author

K.M. Elkes lives and works in the West Country. He has won or been placed in a number of international writing competitions, including the Manchester Fiction Prize, the Bridport Prize, Bath Flash Fiction Award and the Fish Publishing Prize. His short fiction has been published in more than 30 print anthologies in the UK and internationally, as well as literary magazines such as *Unthology*, *The Lonely Crowd*, *Structo* and *Litro*. He is a short story tutor for Comma Press and has led workshops at the UK Flash Fiction Festival and for National Flash Fiction Day. His work has featured on BBC radio and on school and college curricula in the USA, India and China. In 2019, he was the recipient of an Arts Council England award.

Story Index